Night-Night, Little One

BY ANGELA MCALLISTER

ILLUSTRATED BY MAGGIE KNEEN

A Doubleday Book for Young Readers

A Doubleday Book for Young Readers
Published by
Random House Children's Books
a division of Random House, Inc.
1540 Broadway
New York, New York 10036

Doubleday and the anchor with dolphin colophon are registered trademarks of
Random House, Inc.
Text copyright © 2003 by Angela McAllister
Illustrations copyright © 2003 by Maggie Kneen

Visit us on the Web! www.randomhouse.com/kids

Educators and librarians, for a variety of teaching tools, visit us at
www.randomhouse.com/teachers

Library of Congress Cataloging-in-Publication Data
McAllister, Angela.
    Night-night, little one / Angela McAllister ; illustrated by Maggie Kneen.
        p. cm.
    Summary: When Duffy the rabbit does not want to go to sleep, his mother
talks with him until he is tired.
        ISBN: 0-385-32732-3 (trade)
                0-385-90861-X (lib. bdg.)
    [1. Bedtime—Fiction. 2. Mother and child—Fiction. 3. Rabbits—Fiction.]
I. Kneen, Maggie, ill. II. Title.
    PZ7.M11714 Ni 2002
    [E]—dc21   2001053933

The text of this book is set in 16-point Truesdell Bold.
Book design by Trish Parcell Watts
Printed in the United States of America
March 2003
10 9 8 7 6 5 4 3 2 1

To Madeleine
—A.M.

For Joseph and Jack
—M.K.

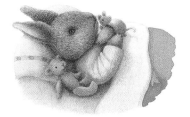

Duffy loved to play in the sunshine with his big sisters.
After breakfast they chased each other into the wood. All day long
they played under the big oak tree, until it was time for supper.

Then, as the sun slipped away, Duffy's sisters helped
him put on his pajamas and they all tumbled into bed.

Mommy read Duffy a story and tucked him in with his cuddly toys.

"Night-night, little one," said Mommy, giving him a kiss. "Sweet dreams." Then she went to see to the girls.

Duffy tried to go to sleep, but something didn't feel right.
He moved his toys around. "Monkey next to Mouse, Big Bear
next to Little Bear, and Duck in the middle," said Duffy.
Something still wasn't right.

"Duck next to Mouse, Big Bear next to Monkey, and
Little Bear in the middle." Duffy made a space for himself
and snuggled down.
    But he couldn't go to sleep.

"Mommy," called Duffy, "can I have a drink of water?"
Mommy brought him a drink. "Go to sleep now. Night-
night, little one." She tucked him in again and closed the door.

Duffy shut his eyes, but
they wanted to be open. He
turned and cuddled Little Bear.

He turned the other way
and cuddled Mouse.

He lay on his back and stared up at the ceiling.

"Mommy," called Duffy, "can I have another story?"
Mommy peeped round the door. "Not now, Duffy,
you're tired," she said. "Go to sleep. Night-night, little one."

Duffy didn't feel tired. He sang a quiet song to Monkey, but it got louder and louder.

Mommy came back again. "Duffy, sing quietly or you'll keep everyone awake."

"But monkey songs aren't quiet," explained Duffy.

"Then sing a monkey lullaby," said Mommy with a frown. "Go to sleep now. Night-night, little one."

"But I'm not tired," said Duffy. "I'm lonely, and I don't like the dark."

Mommy sat down on his bed. She gave Duffy a big hug, and he yawned. "You are tired," she said.

"But I'm still lonely."

"You've got all your friends here," Mommy said. "Big Bear and Little Bear, Monkey, Mouse, and Duck."

"But we don't like the nighttime," said Duffy. "It's so quiet, and nothing happens in the dark."

Mommy opened the curtains. Stars twinkled in the sky. "It's only at night that you can see the stars," she said.

Duffy liked the stars. "But who sees them if everyone is asleep?" he asked.

"Oh, the night is a busy time," said Mommy.
"Mr. Fox takes his walk."

"The Hedgehog family is out looking for snails."

"Mrs. Bat teaches her children to fly,
and moths love to dance in the starlight."

"Then, of course, there's Mrs. Badger. . . ."

"Does she dance in the starlight?" asked Duffy, giggling.
"No," said Mommy with a laugh. "She has to get little
Herbert and his sisters up and give them breakfast."

"Breakfast at nighttime?" asked Duffy.
"That's right," said Mommy.
"Then the children chase each other into the wood."

"Into my wood?" asked Duffy.
"Yes, but at night it's Herbert's wood.
All night they play under the big oak tree."
"Under my oak tree?" asked Duffy.

"Yes, but at night it's Herbert's oak tree,"
said Mommy. She plumped up Duffy's pillow.
"But when does Herbert go to sleep?" asked
Duffy, trying hard to keep his eyes open.

"When the morning comes, Mrs. Badger puts Herbert
to bed with all his cuddly toys and tucks him in."

"Does she read him a story?" asked Duffy with a yawn.

"Of course," said Mommy.

"Does she give him a drink?"

"Of course," said Mommy.

"And does he go to sleep?" Duffy asked with a really big yawn.

"No," said Mommy. "He calls out to Mrs. Badger and says, 'I'm not tired, and I'm lonely, and I don't like the daytime.'"

"That's silly," said Duffy with the biggest yawn of all.

"Yes, how silly," agreed Mommy.
She gave Duffy a kiss.

"And Mrs. Badger gives Herbert a kiss and says,
'Day-day, little one.'"

"Day-day," Duffy said with a
sleepy smile. "I love you, Mommy."
     "I love you, too."

And as the moon slipped its night-light
into Duffy's bedroom, he fell fast asleep.